Amelia Bedelia
· Tries Her Luck ·

by **Herman Parish** ✿ pictures by **Lynne Avril**

HOORAY!

_____

can read this book!

I Can Read!

BEGINNING 1 READING

Amelia Bedelia
·Tries Her Luck·

by Herman Parish ✿ pictures by Lynne Avril

Greenwillow Books, *An Imprint of* HarperCollins*Publishers*

Amelia Bedelia was getting ready

to go to school when . . .

CRASH!

"I'm sorry!" said Amelia Bedelia.

"Accidents happen, sweetie,"
said her mother.

"The important thing
is that you are not hurt."

At school, Amelia Bedelia told her friends
about the accident.

"You're in trouble," said Clay.

"Breaking a mirror means

seven years of bad luck."

"Seven years!"

said Amelia Bedelia.

"That's almost my whole life!"

"Even worse," said Rose.

"Today is Friday the thirteenth.

Bad luck gets doubled today."

"That's fourteen years!"

said Amelia Bedelia.

"I'll have bad luck forever!"

9

"Amelia Bedelia," said Joy,

"you can change your luck."

"That's right," said Heather.

"My dad always says,

See a penny, pick it up,

all the day you'll have good luck."

Amelia Bedelia picked up Penny.

"Put me down!" said Penny.

"Heather means a penny coin,

not a Penny person."

At recess, the whole class
tried to help Amelia Bedelia
change her luck.

They searched
for a four-leaf clover.

They looked for
a lucky horseshoe.

They tried to find a rabbit's foot.

The playground didn't have any of those things.

"I'm sorry, Amelia Bedelia," said Clay. "We struck out. You are out of luck."

Amelia Bedelia made a plan.

If she could not find luck,

she would make her own luck.

Two Rabbit's Feet = Double Luck

12 Leaf Clover = 3 × Luck

ur Horseshoes = 4 × Luck

15

Amelia Bedelia's teacher, Miss Edwards,

saw her drawings.

She also saw that Amelia Bedelia was upset.

"Are you all right?" asked Miss Edwards.

"No, I am all wrong,"
said Amelia Bedelia.
She told Miss Edwards
about breaking the mirror
and her double bad luck.

"Amelia Bedelia," said Miss Edwards, "today is my lucky day. Friday the thirteenth is the perfect day to talk about luck."

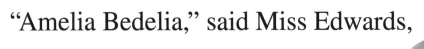

The class listed lucky and unlucky things.

They talked about bad luck and good luck.

There were all kinds of questions.

Good Luck

4 Leaf Clover
Horseshoe
Blowing out candles on
birthday Cake

Miss Edwards told the class a story.

"When I was your age," she said,

"One saying really scared me.

It was, *Step on a crack,*

break your mother's back."

21

"That's terrible," said Amelia Bedelia.

"But it isn't true," said Miss Edwards.

"Just like breaking a mirror isn't bad luck."

"Breaking a mirror is bad luck," said Clay.

"It's bad luck for the mirror!"

Everyone laughed.

Amelia Bedelia laughed hardest of all.

She felt a lot better.

As Amelia Bedelia was walking home,

she saw a crack in the sidewalk.

"Bad luck? Ha!" she said.

She stepped on the crack.

She stepped on every crack she saw.

When she spied the biggest one of all,

Amelia Bedelia stomped on it.

Then Amelia Bedelia turned onto her street, and she stopped in her tracks.

There was an ambulance

in front of her house.

Amelia Bedelia raced home.

Breaking the mirror was an accident,

but she had stepped on those cracks

on purpose.

"Mom!" yelled Amelia Bedelia.

"I didn't mean to break your back!"

The ambulance was pulling away.

"Mom!" cried Amelia Bedelia. "Mom!"

"Amelia Bedelia!" said her mother.

"I'm with Mrs. Adams, sweetie."

Amelia Bedelia whirled around.

Her mom was with their neighbor.

Her back was fine!

Amelia Bedelia ran to her mom.

She gave her the biggest,

longest, strongest hug ever.

"Ouch, honey!"

said Amelia Bedelia's mother.

"Do you want to break my back?"

"No, never!" said Amelia Bedelia.

"You just missed the excitement,"
said Mrs. Adams.

"I got a ride home in an ambulance
after my checkup."

"Are you okay?" asked Amelia Bedelia.

"I am fine," said Mrs. Adams.

"Knock on wood."

Then Mrs. Adams knocked three times
on her porch railing.

Tomorrow, Amelia Bedelia would add
"knock on wood" to the list
her class had made.
Today, worrying about luck
had worn her out.

Amelia Bedelia thought about
her family and her great friends.
She thought that the mirror
Mrs. Adams gave her was cool.

Amelia Bedelia felt like she was
the luckiest person in the world.